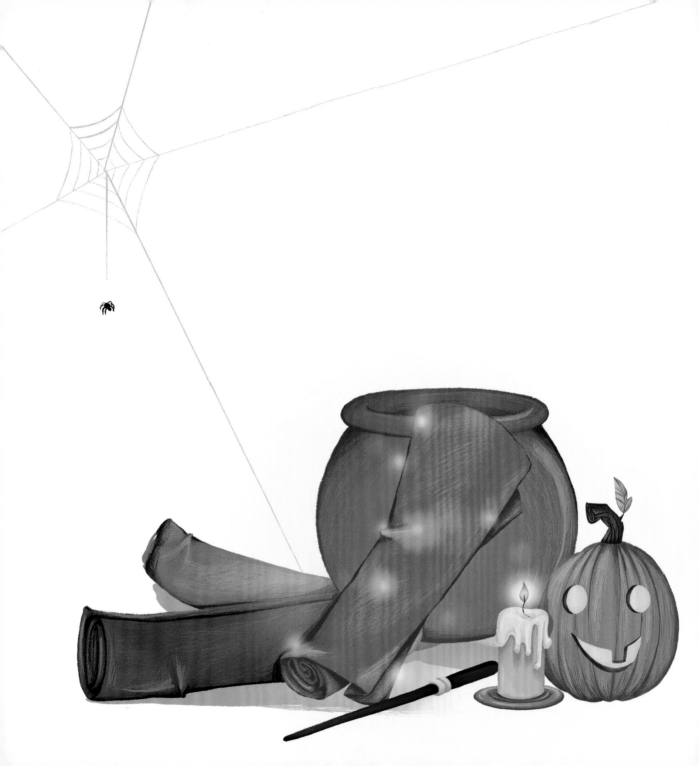

THE secret HALLOWEEN COSTUME

Text: Sophie Vaillancourt • Illustrations: Karina Dupuis
Translation: John Conn

CRACKBOOM!

October has finally arrived. It's Charlotte's favorite time of the year: Halloween! The little witch is helping her parents put up decorations.
But Charlotte is distracted…

"Mom," she asks, "do I have to be a scary witch on Halloween? Can't I be something different?"

"Now, Charlotte," answers her mom. "Everyone knows that witches have to be scary on Halloween. It's tradition!"

Charlotte groans. This tradition stinks!

The next day, Charlotte meets her friends Elena and Ruby at the park. They can tell she's unhappy. "What's wrong?" asks Elena. "My mom wants me to be a scary witch for Halloween, as usual," says Charlotte. "But I don't like scaring people."

Elena and Ruby are surprised. Little witches have always worn scary costumes at Halloween. It's a tradition. But there must be a way to help Charlotte.
"We could go through the trunks in my attic," suggests Ruby. "We might find something there."
"Great idea!" exclaim Charlotte and Elena.

In Ruby's attic, the three little witches discover a trunk filled with costumes and props. Elena and Ruby sort through them, looking for something Charlotte might like.

Ruby tries on a cape. "What do you think? Vampires are cool." "I won't be able to talk wearing plastic fangs!" says Charlotte.

Elena takes a fuzzy costume from the trunk.
"What about a werewolf?"

"I'm going to be too hot under all that fur!"
says Charlotte. "Besides, these costumes are
all too scary."

Charlotte had really hoped to find a new costume, and she's feeling discouraged—until she notices a roll of red fabric in the corner of the attic.

"Ruby, can I take this fabric to Grandma Lily?" she asks. "Of course," Ruby says.

Charlotte is so excited she runs all the way to Grandma Lily's house.

Grandma Lily is a bit of an eccentric witch. She does things her own way and doesn't care about tradition. Some people find her strange, but Charlotte thinks she's one of the most interesting witches she's ever met. She loves her grandmother.

"What a lovely surprise!" Grandma Lily exclaims.

"Grandma Lily, I don't want to follow the Halloween tradition anymore," says Charlotte. "I don't want to be scary. Can you help me?"

"Of course!" says her grandma. "I love anything that's out of the ordinary."

Charlotte whispers her secret idea to her grandmother, and Grandma Lily springs into action.

When Halloween finally arrives, Charlotte wears her black dress to school, as usual. But unlike her classmates, she doesn't wear scary makeup.

She takes a long piece of red cloth out of her backpack and knots it around her neck. Her witch's hat is decorated in a matching shade of red.

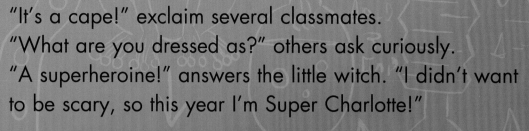

"It's a cape!" exclaim several classmates.
"What are you dressed as?" others ask curiously.
"A superheroine!" answers the little witch. "I didn't want
to be scary, so this year I'm Super Charlotte!"

Charlotte takes other costumes out of her bag:
cat ears, a pirate hat, fairy wings…
"No one has to be scary for Halloween,"
she declares. "Everyone should wear whatever
they like!"

Her classmates cheer.
Mr. Pumpkin, their teacher, is a little taken aback.
But he smiles and is soon won over by his students'
enthusiasm. So much for tradition!
"What a great idea, Charlotte!" he says.
"Children, you are free to wear
any costume you like."

Charlotte's classmates try on the costumes she has brought. She couldn't be happier with her own costume. From now on, listening to her heart will be Charlotte's new tradition!

CrackBoom! Books is an imprint of Chouette Publishing (1987) Inc.

Text: Sophie Vaillancourt
All rights reserved.
Illustrations: Karina Dupuis
Translation: John Conn

Chouette Publishing would like to thank the Government of Canada and SODEC
for their financial support.

Bibliothèque et Archives nationales du Québec and Library and Archives Canada cataloguing in
publication

Title: The secret Halloween costume / text: Sophie Vaillancourt; illustrations: Karina Dupuis; translation:
John Conn.

Other titles: Costume secret d'Halloween. English

Names: Vaillancourt, Sophie, 1991- author. | Dupuis, Karina, 1982- illustrator.
| Conn, John, translator.

Description: Translation of: Le costume secret d'Halloween.

Identifiers: Canadiana 20210045647 | ISBN 9782898022456 (hardcover)

Classification: LCC PS8643.A3664 C6713 2021 | DDC jC843/.6—dc23

Legal deposit – Bibliothèque et Archives nationales du Québec, 2021.
Legal deposit – Library and Archives Canada, 2021.

Printed in Dongguan, China
10 9 8 7 6 5 4 3 2 1   CHO2126 MAR2021

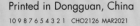